The Lemonade Guitar

Brady Schenk, with Riley & Graham Schenk
Illustrated by: Andrew Laitinen

LUCIDBOOKS

The Lemonade Guitar

Copyright © 2021 by Brady Schenk, with Riley & Graham Schenk
Illustrated by Andrew Laitinen

Published by Lucid Books in Houston, TX
www.LucidBooksPublishing.com

ISBN 978-1-63296-469-4 (paperback)
ISBN 978-1-63296-471-7 (hardback)
ISBN 978-1-63296-470-0 (ebook)

Special Sales: Most Lucid Books titles are available in special quantity discounts. Custom imprinting or excerpting can also be done to fit special needs. For standard bulk orders, go to www.lucidbooksbulk.com. For specialty press or large orders, contact Lucid Books at books@lucidbookspublishing.com.

Riley and Graham rushed out of the dugout
for family dinner with Mama and Papa.

The line at their favorite pizza place stretched out the door.

"Mama, are they going to run out of pizza?" Graham asked

"I could eat a horse! I'm so hungry!" Riley's tummy growled

As they stood in line, people walked past them into the store next door.

It had been empty a long time.

Riley peeked through the store window and gasped.

His hunger vanished.

Drums! Pianos!

Riley's eyes raced through the new music store.

"There!" he said to himself.
On the back wall he saw
what he was looking for.

"Guitars!

Could there be one my size?" he wondered.

As he turned to ask to go inside, Riley heard
Graham call, "Riley, on a hop! It's our turn!"

At their table, Papa bent waxy sticks into fun glasses.
Riley and Graham put them on and giggled.

Graham drummed his hands on the table and said,

"Look, Mama. We could be in a band!"

Riley pretended to play a guitar.

"Papa, could you buy us real drums and a guitar?" Riley asked.

Papa laughed and said, "Why don't you buy them yourselves?"

"Silly Papa. We don't have any money," said Graham.

"Well, what could you do to earn some?" Mama asked.

"When you learn how to earn money, you can have your own."

The pizza arrived. Papa gave each boy a slice,
but now Riley wanted a guitar more than food.
"Earning money comes from serving others," said Papa.
"What is something of value you can offer to others in exchange for money?"

omething of value?" Riley asked. "Like my toys?"

ure," Papa said. "You have exchanged your money for a toy before."

ell my toys?" Riley couldn't imagine it.

Why not? Some people sell toys.

ome sell pizza. Some sell horses.

ght, Graham?"

emonade! That's something of value! Kids walking home from school would love
cold cup of lemonade. We could serve them by selling it. Would it work, Papa?"
emonade seems valuable to Graham," Papa answered. "Sometimes we have to
e it a shot and work things out as we learn more."

"Let's go to the music store and see if they have instruments your size," Papa said. Riley scarfed down the rest of his pizza. He blasted through the music store doors, ready for a treasure hunt for the perfect guitar.

his surprise, a woman with green-and-purple hair and tattoos down one arm
ked to help him. Riley stood speechless.

"Welcome to my music store! I'm Ariana. How can I help you?" Papa nudged Riley.

Seeing Riley's surprise, she continued. "I love sharing
the gift of music making. What are you looking for?"
"A drum set!" shouted Graham.
"And . . . a guitar! Do you have small guitars?" Riley finally had the courage to ask
"Absolutely." With Ariana's help, the boys found the perfect guitar and drum set

Holding his future guitar, Riley couldn't wait to start earning money selling lemonade.

He asked, "Papa, how many cups will I have to sell to buy this guitar?" Mama corrected him. "You mean, how many customers will you have to serve? As many as it takes."

On the way home, Graham saw a brand-new sports car.
"Hey, Riley. I'm excited for you to get a guitar,
but I may pass on the drum set." Riley didn't reply.

The sweet sounds of guitar strings at
his fingertips were all he could hear.

The next day was blazing hot. As they carried lemonade and cups to a table in the front yard, Graham asked, "Papa, how much will each cup cost?"

"Great question!" said Papa. "Do you mean to make it or buy it?"

"It costs us to make it?" asked Riley.

Papa explained, "We bought the cups and lemonade. We spent time and energy to make the lemonade, set up, and sell it, right?"

"Goodness!" Riley said. "Will the lemonade cost too much for kids to buy?"

Papa answered, "We need to charge more than it costs us, but not too much. Let's see if they will buy each cup for 25 cents."

"ounds good, Papa," said Graham. "Say, how much did you pay for the house?"

apa laughed. "Graham, your ideas keep getting bigger and bigger."

ley looked concerned. "Are you sure 25 cents is enough?"

No," said Papa. "But remember, we can try this and then change

we need to. Here comes your first customer."

"Are you selling lemonade?" asked a girl. Riley froze.

"Well, are you?" Papa asked.

Riley couldn't speak. He remembered the music store owner. What had she said?

"Yes!" said Riley. "How can I help you?"

"One cup, please," she said.

raham was ready. "It costs 25 cents."

landing Graham a dollar, she said, "My mom said keep the change."

Really?" said Riley.

apa poured the lemonade. He handed her the cup. "How is it?"

Mmmm!" she said. "Really good!"

Boys, what do y'all tell your happy customer?"

"Thank you!" Riley and Graham said together.

A mom with a baby walked up. She paid with a $5 bill.

"Keep the change," she said.

The afternoon and two more pitchers of lemonade went by quickly.
Riley felt good serving others. He was earning money
for his guitar one cup at a time.

Sometimes Papa gave cups of lemonade away for free
to thirsty kids who didn't have 25 cents.

"Why, Papa? It doesn't get me closer to my guitar," said Riley.

"The plans of the diligent lead to prosperity," quoted Papa.

"If we keep working, we will earn enough. When we are generous,
we imitate God, who gave us something we couldn't buy ourselves."

That night, Papa counted the money they earned and made three stacks.
"The first stack we give to someone in need. The second stack is for supplies.
The third stack is profit. Since you are both business owners,
you each get to keep half."

or weeks, Riley and Graham sold lemonade on hot afternoons.
ustomers loved hearing about Riley's guitar and Graham's house with a pool.
How many cups of lemonade does it take to make a guitar?" asked a customer.
iley smiled. "As many as it takes! I get closer with each customer we serve."

Two thousand, three hundred and seven cups of lemonade later, Graham and Riley
marched through the doors of the music store like kings!
Ariana cheered. "Back for your dream guitar and drum set?" she asked them.
Riley felt thankful for working hard through so many hot,
sweaty days serving others. Mama called this perseverance.

Then Riley said, "Since last time, we sold 2,307 cups of lemonade to hundreds of customers. We learned about costs, profits, and generosity. This is no dream guitar. This is the Lemonade Guitar! It's better than a dream because I earned it."

Ariana was shocked to hear a boy talk so much like a man. As she turned to ask Graham about his drums, he said, "I've decided to hold off on the drums. I'm saving my profits for things down the road."

Riley gladly exchanged some of his money for a guitar, a case, and extra strings.
The boys were happy they had learned how to earn money by serving others.

When they got home with Riley's Lemonade Guitar, Graham squeezed between Mama and Papa on the couch. "Yes, Graham?" asked Papa.
"About my private jet . . ."
"Do you really want a jet, Graham?" asked Riley as he picked his guitar strings.

For sure! But I will need other things in the future too. Now I know something f great value. Papa, will you help me write a book about two brothers who arn to earn their own money? I've got a great title for it."

The lemonade Guitar

Brady Schenk grew up in the agricultural setting of the Texas Panhandle with two loving parents, three smart and athletic older sisters, and a caring community of extended family and friends. Life instilled in him a sense of integrity and a strong work ethic that led to progressive success academically, athletically, and socially. He played and coached baseball at the college and international levels before earning his Master of Business Administration from Northeastern University with a dual emphasis in finance and entrepreneurship. Brady and his wife, Megan (married in 2004), have two sons, Riley and Graham, and reside in the Texas Panhandle, where Brady helps families form and shape their future realities.

CPSIA information can be obtained
at www.ICGtesting.com
Printed in the USA
BVHW021215190821
614777BV00006B/454